Maisy's Bathtime

Lucy Cousins

WALKER BOOKS
AND SUBSIDIARIES

LONDON • BOSTON • SYDNEY • AUCKLAND

It's Maisy's bathtime.

She runs the water and puts in some bubbles ...

and in goes Duck.

Ding-dong!
Oh, that's
the doorbell.

Maisy runs downstairs to see who it is.

Hello, Tallulah.

Maisy can't play now, it's her bathtime.

Maisy runs back upstairs and gets undressed.

Maisy jumps in the bubbly bath.

Ding-dong! Who is ringing the doorbell now?

It's Tallulah again.

Maisy's having her bath now. Come and play later, Tallulah.

Oh! Where are you going, Tallulah?

Tallulah goes to the bathroom and takes off her clothes.

Splash, splash!

Maisy and Tallulah play in the bath.

Hooray!

Read and enjoy the Maisy story books

Maisy Dresses Up

A Maisy Story Book Lucy Cousins

Maisy's Bedtime

A Maisy Story Book Lucy Cousins

Maisy's Pool

A Maisy Story Book Lucy Cousins

Maisy Makes Lemonade

A Maisy Story Book Lucy Cousins

Maisy's Bus

A Maisy Story Book Lucy Cousins

Maisy Tidies Up

A Maisy Story Book Lucy Cousins

Maisy Makes Gingerbread

A Maisy Story Book Lucy Cousins

Maisy's Bathtime

A Maisy Story Book Lucy Cousins

My friend Maisy

Doctor Maisy

A Maisy Story Book Lucy Cousins

Maisy Goes Shopping

A Maisy Story Book Lucy Cousins

Available from all good booksellers

It's more fun with Maisy!